Annie and Snowball and the Thankful Friends

The Tenth Book of Their Adventures

Cynthia Rylant

Illustrated by Suçie Stevenson

READY-TO-READ

SIMON SPOTLIGHT

New York   London   Toronto   Sydney   New Delhi

For Bernice Carew, Maggie, and Nellie
—S. S.

SIMON SPOTLIGHT
An imprint of Simon & Schuster Children's Publishing Division
1230 Avenue of the Americas, New York, New York 10020
Text copyright © 2011 by Cynthia Rylant
Illustrations copyright © 2011 by Suçie Stevenson

For information about special discounts for bulk purchases, please contact
Simon & Schuster Special Sales at 1-866-506-1949 or business@simonandschuster.com.
The Simon & Schuster Speakers Bureau can bring authors to your live event. For more
information or to book an event contact the Simon & Schuster Speakers Bureau at
1-866-248-3049 or visit our website at www.simonspeakers.com.
Designed by Tom Daly
The text of this book was set in Goudy Old Style.
The illustrations for this book were rendered in pen-and-ink and watercolor.
Manufactured in the United States of America 0812 LAK
First Simon Spotlight paperback edition September 2012
2 4 6 8 10 9 7 5 3 1
The Library of Congress has cataloged the hardcover edition as follows:
Rylant, Cynthia.
Annie and Snowball and the thankful friends: the tenth book of their adventures /
By Cynthia Rylant ; illustrated by Suçie Stevenson.
p. cm. — (Ready-to-read)
Summary: Annie wants to fill every chair in her house's dining room for Thanksgiving
dinner, and asks for her friend Henry's help in thinking of people to invite.
[1. Thanksgiving Day—Fiction. 2. Neighborliness—Fiction.] I. Stevenson, Suçie, ill.
II. Title.
PZ7.R982Anu 2011
[E]—dc22
2010018473
ISBN 978-1-4169-7202-0 (pbk)
ISBN 978-1-4169-7200-6 (hc)
ISBN 978-1-4169-8252-4 (eBook)

Contents

A Big Table

It was almost time for Thanksgiving.
Annie loved Thanksgiving.
This year she wanted to have a big
dinner in her new neighborhood.

Her cousin Henry lived next door,
and Annie knew that his family would
come for dinner at her house.

But who else could Annie
and her dad invite?
Annie didn't have any brothers or sisters.
She didn't have a big family of her own.

But there was a big table in her house,
and she wanted *lots* of people around it.
Who could she invite for Thanksgiving?

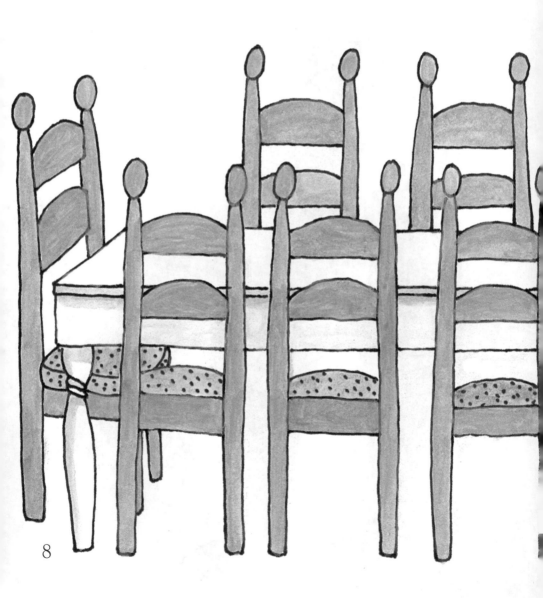

Good Ideas

Annie counted the dining room chairs. Then she and her bunny, Snowball, went next door to visit Henry.

Henry was playing cards
with his big dog, Mudge.
Mudge was winning because
he was drooling on the cards.

Henry didn't want drooly cards,
so Mudge got to keep the drooly ones.
Mudge had a lot of cards!

Annie sat next to Henry.

"We have room for five more people
for Thanksgiving dinner," she told Henry.

"Great!" said Henry.
"But I don't know anyone else
to invite," said Annie.

"Hmm," said Henry.

Henry always had good ideas about dogs.

But he wasn't sure he had good ideas
about dinners.

"Does your grandmother have
any old friends?" asked Henry.
"That's a great idea!" said Annie.
"We can invite her two best friends."

"And what about the postman, Mr. Bell?"
said Henry. "His family lives in Alaska."
"You're right!" said Annie. "Maybe he'd
like to have dinner with us."

"And maybe Miss Chan," said Henry.

"Of course!" said Annie.

Miss Chan taught first grade
at their school.

She was from China.

Her family was far away, too.

"Great!" said Henry. "That's four.
But didn't you say you have
five extra chairs?"

"Yes," said Annie. "But I can't think of
anyone else to invite."

"Hmm," said Henry.

"Maybe someone else will just show up."

23

Pretty Cards

Annie asked her dad if she could invite
more people for Thanksgiving dinner.
He said, "Sure!"
So she made little cards.

She gave two to her grandmother,
one to Mr. Bell, and one to Miss Chan.

The cards had sparkly orange glitter
on them and pictures of fall leaves
and many hearts.
Please join us for Thanksgiving,
the cards said.

Annie hoped everyone would.

Thankful!

On Thanksgiving Day, Annie was
very excited.
She dressed up in an orange corduroy
jumper and orange tights
and brown shiny shoes.

"I want to look pumpkin-y," Annie told her dad.
Snowball looked pumpkin-y too.
She was wearing a sparkly orange bow.

Annie set the table
while her dad cooked the dinner.
Annie brought out all her favorite
teapots and teacups.

She made place cards and set them
in little pinecones.

She gathered fall leaves in a big basket
for the table.
It all looked beautiful.

Then everyone arrived.

Grandmother's friends met Snowball
and Mudge.

Mr. Bell met Miss Chan.

Everyone new met everyone old.
Then they all sat down to eat.

Annie said the blessing:
"We give thanks for good food
and good family and good friends.
We give thanks for snowy bunnies
and drooly dogs.
We give thanks for everything."

Then her dad carved the turkey, and
they all had a wonderful dinner.

And *just* as they were finishing up,
who walked through the front door?
"Aunt Sally!" said Annie and Henry.

She was a surprise.
She had flown all the way from
California.
And she had crackers and carrots
in her pockets.
Annie's dad pulled the eleventh chair
to the table.

"I am *thankful* you haven't eaten *everything*!" said Aunt Sally. Then they all had a second helping as Thanksgiving dinner started all over again!